To my cousin, a treasure so rare,
together we play, dream, and dare.
In laughter and fun, our spirits soar,
a big 'ol world out there to explore!

With dreams as vast as ocean's tide,
we'll sail through life, side by side.
In every giggle, every grin,
our bond grows deeper, from within.

In fields of green and skies so blue,
with laughter echoing, just us two.
We'll chase the wind and climb the trees,
our hearts alive with endless glee.

In secret forts, we'll make our stand,
defenders of our own small land.
With sticks for swords and dreams as shields,
adventure calls, across the fields.

So, here's my vow, steadfast and sincere,
a friendly embrace, enduring and dear.
Through all life's twists, no matter the way,
my cousin, my friend, forever you'll stay.

Love,
Your cousin

At the park, we'll swing high and slide low,
chasing dreams wherever we go.

With sandy toes and salty air,
beach days with you are beyond compare.

Under the stars, by the fire's glow,
our camping adventures steal the show.

With balloons, cake, and presents too,
birthday parties are the best with you.

In costumes bright and colors bold,
our dress-up parties are a sight to behold.

Make some popcorn and dim the light,
then we'll settle in for movie night!

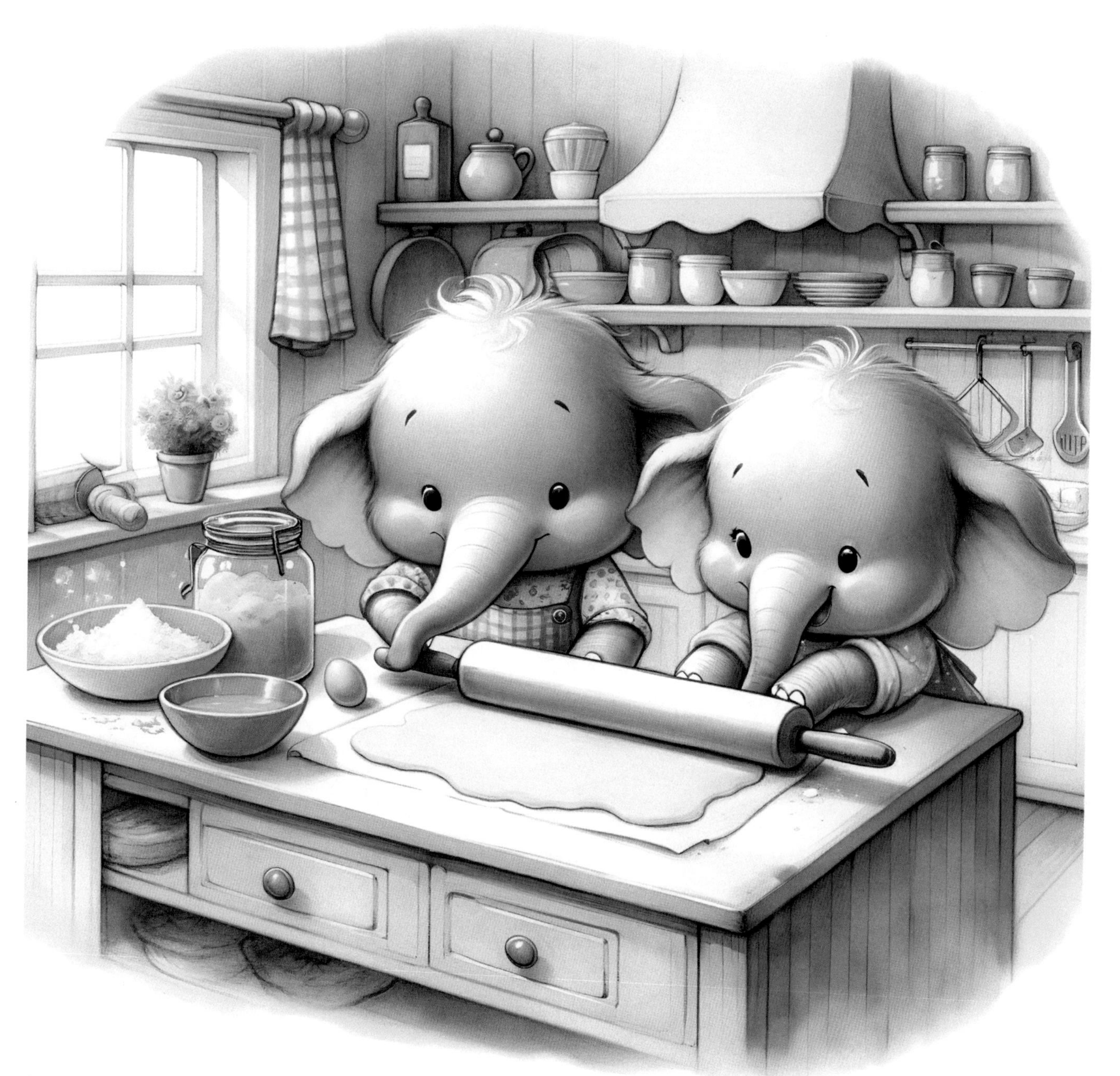

With flour on our noses and smiles so sweet,
baking cookies with you is such a treat.

When snowflakes fall and the world turns white,
our snow day adventures are such a delight.

With curiosity bubbling and mess on our minds,
our science experiments are one-of-a-kind.

Our giggles will float through sunlit air,
and blossoms will bloom with love and care.

Together we'll jam and create a song,
through laughter and harmony, all day long.

Dipped in colors, our brushes will glide,
day to night, we'll create with pride.

With baseballs flying and goals to score,
sports with you are never a bore.

Beneath the trees, with skies so blue,
picnics with you are a dream come true.

There's history to uncover and wonders to see,
museum exploration will set our minds free.

With the wind in our hair and sights to behold,
road trips like this are a story untold.

With apples to pick, so crisp and so sweet,
we'll make special memories that can't be beat.

In our backyard, with imaginations wide,
we'll pretend to be pirates, stand side by side.

Bundled up cozy, in layers so tight,
cousins together in the soft winter light.

With whispers in trees and secrets to explore,
in an magical forest, we'll find so much more.

Together we'll groove, two-step and slide,
cousins in rhythm, our spirits collide.

We'll go on a journey, so free and so true,
an epic adventure for just me and you.

With you by my side, the world feels small.
Together, I know, we can conquer it all!

So here's my promise, so honest and deep,
a bond of friendship, will be ours to keep.
For all of our days, it'll be you and me.
my cousin and friend, you forever will be.

a little note for my special cousin

Made in the USA
Middletown, DE
21 December 2024